# Saturday Popular Concerts.

DIRECTOR—Mr. S. ARTHUR CHAPPELL.

## Five Hundred and First Concert.*

PROGRAMME FROM THE WORKS OF

# Various Masters.

SATURDAY AFTERNOON, JANUARY 23rd, 1875.

* Sixteenth Concert of the Seventeenth Season.

QUARTET, in C major, Op. 20, No. 2, for two Violins, Viola, and Violoncello. *Haydn.*

(Second performance at the Popular Concerts.)

Moderato—C major.
Adagio—C minor; with Episode—E flat major.
Minuetto—C major; with Trio—C minor.
Allegro (Finale—Fuga a quattro suggetti)—C major.

Madame NORMAN-NÉRUDA,
Herr L. RIES, Herr STRAUS, and Signor PIATTI.

This quartet is, in many respects, one of the most original and curious of the almost countless examples of chamber music its inexhaustible composer has given to art. Each movement has a strongly marked character of its own.

*Moderato* (leading theme).

The first violin, hitherto tacit, now takes up the theme, in the dominant:—

(Melody only.)

Again the second violin takes up the theme in the primary key, but with certain modifications :—

Thence we get speedily into the region of the orthodox dominant, as a preparation for the second theme.

This second theme is made up of a diversity of phrases, as, for example :—

And then, after a full close :—

Then again :—

Then once more :—

Then an episode in an extraneous key (E flat) :—

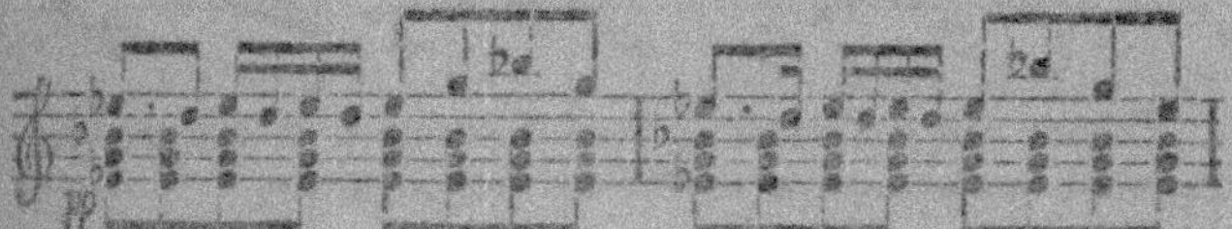


And, lastly, the playful peroration in the dominant (G) :—

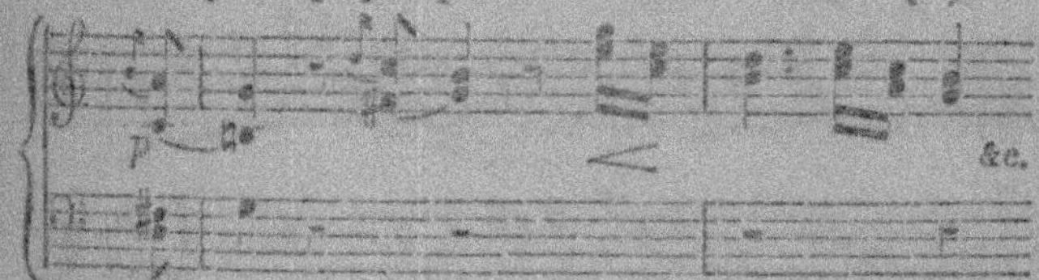


The second part begins with an episode :—

—which, after being led through a variety of keys, gives way to some interesting development of the materials already cited. These return with some unimportant changes, after the accustomed manner. The episode to the second theme comes now in A flat (instead of E flat):—

(Melody only.)

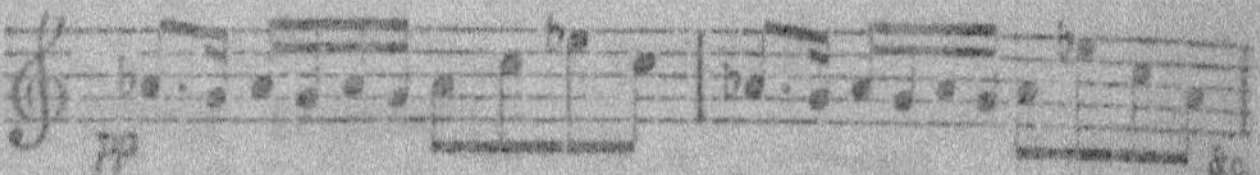

—and the movement thus tranquilly comes to a close.

The charm of this *moderato* lies in its exquisite and tuneful simplicity. Both first and second sections are intended by the composer to be repeated.

*Adagio* (leading theme).

The four instruments in unison.

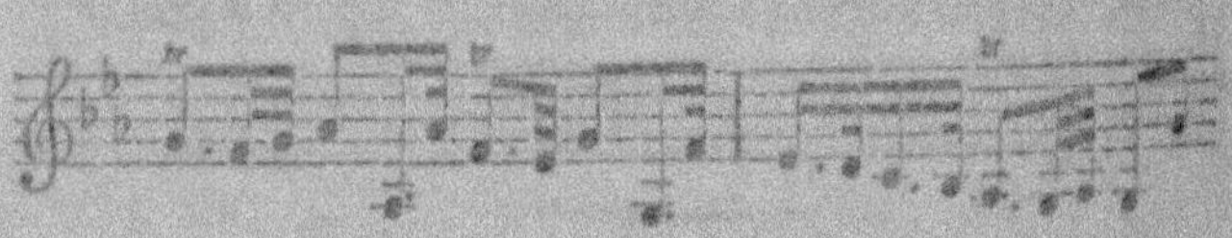

The violoncello then takes the theme:—

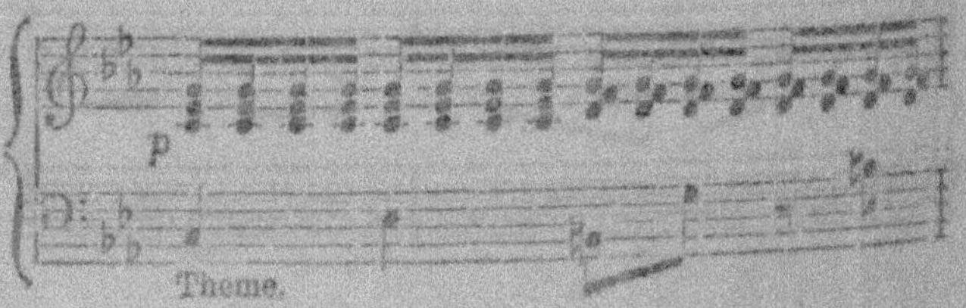

&c.
(Tributary.)
decres.
&c.
(Episode—E flat major.)
The Viola here plays an accompaniment of triplets in arpeggio.
&c.

It is not requisite to quote further from this brief, but fine movement, in which Haydn makes freer use of unison than is his ordinary custom. It does not come to a full close, but breaks off on the harmony of the dominant, thus introducing the *minuetto*, in C major:—

*Minuetto.*

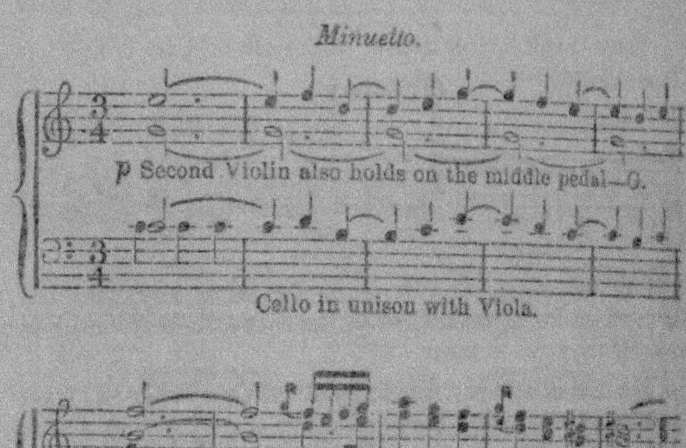


At the end of the first section of the *minuetto*, we have again the four instruments in unison:—

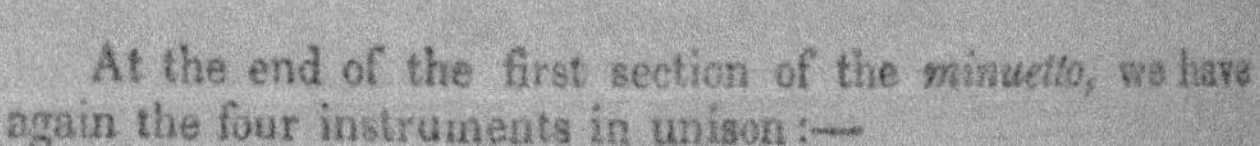

*Trio* (C minor).

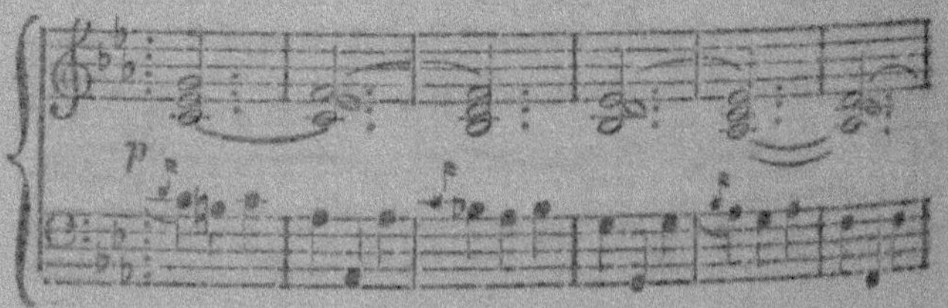

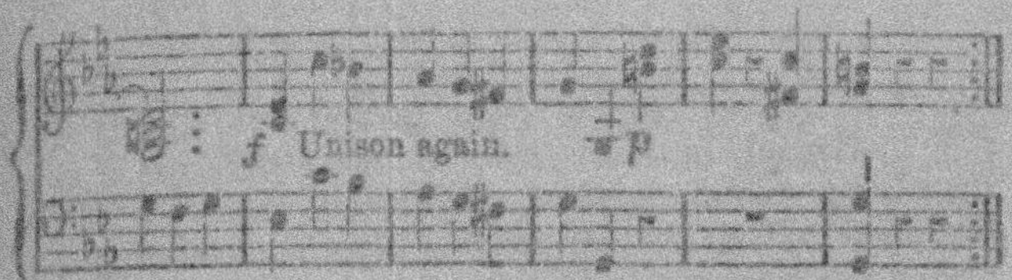


There is still further unison in the second part of this *trio*. Thus it begins :—

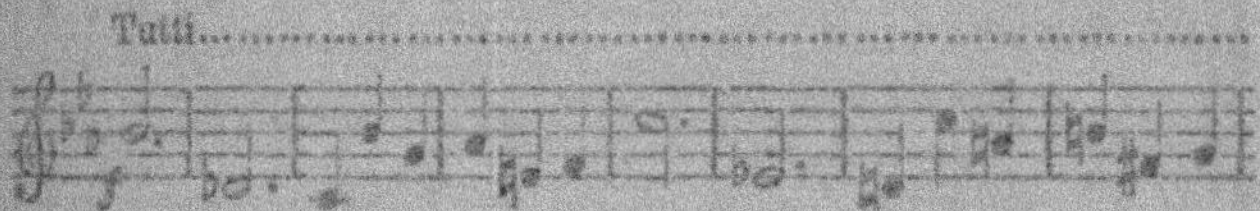


Like the *adagio* (which is in the same key), the *trio* leaves off on the dominant, when the *minuetto* is resumed in precisely the same manner.

The final *allegro* is a free but elaborately-conducted fugue, built upon the four themes subjoined :—

(First theme—First Violin.)

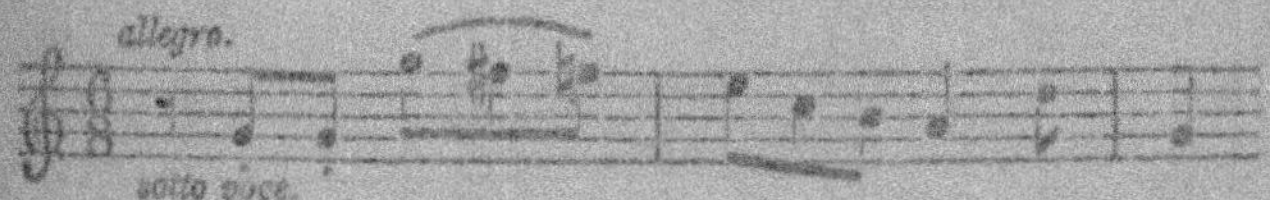


(Second theme—Viola.)

(Third theme—First Violin.)

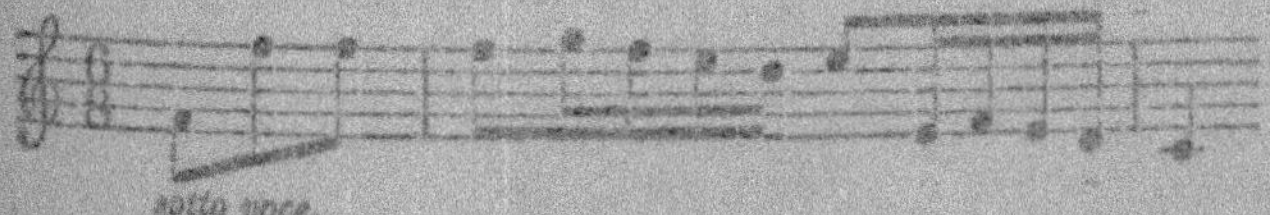


(Fourth theme—Viola.)

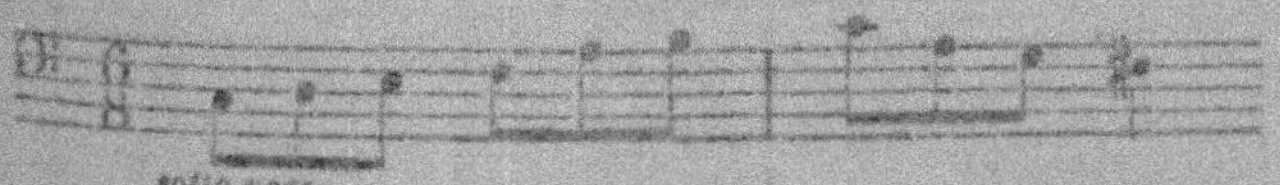

It will be observed that each theme begins on a different part of the bar. Theme 1 is answered, at the fourth bar, by the second violin, a fifth below:—

Theme 2, at the sixth bar, by the first violin, a fifth above:—

Theme 3, at the seventh bar, by the second violin, a fourth below:

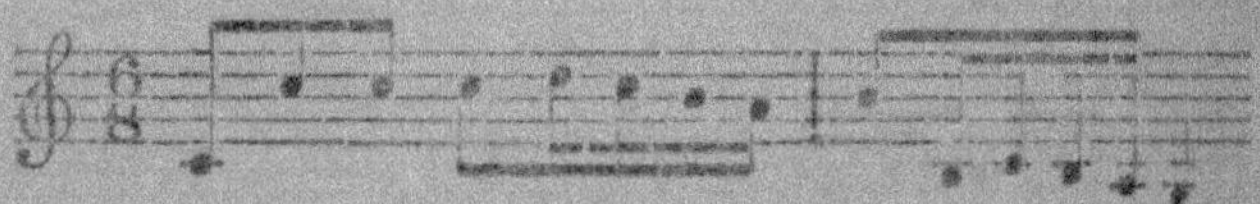

Theme 4, at the eighth bar, by the first violin, a fifth above:—

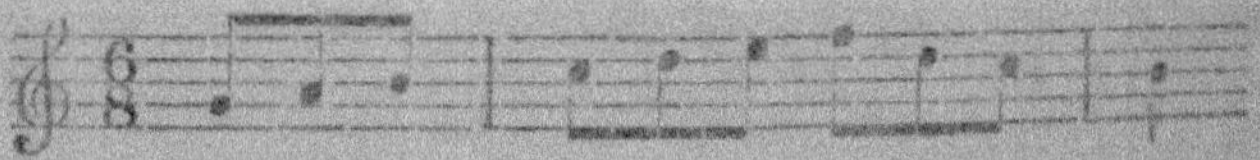

It should now be shown how Haydn makes them assort, as counterpoint to each other. Thus he sets out:—

No. 2.
No. 1.
No. 4.

No. 4.
No. 3.
No. 2.
No. 1.

Accompaniment.
No. 4.
No. 3.
No. 1.

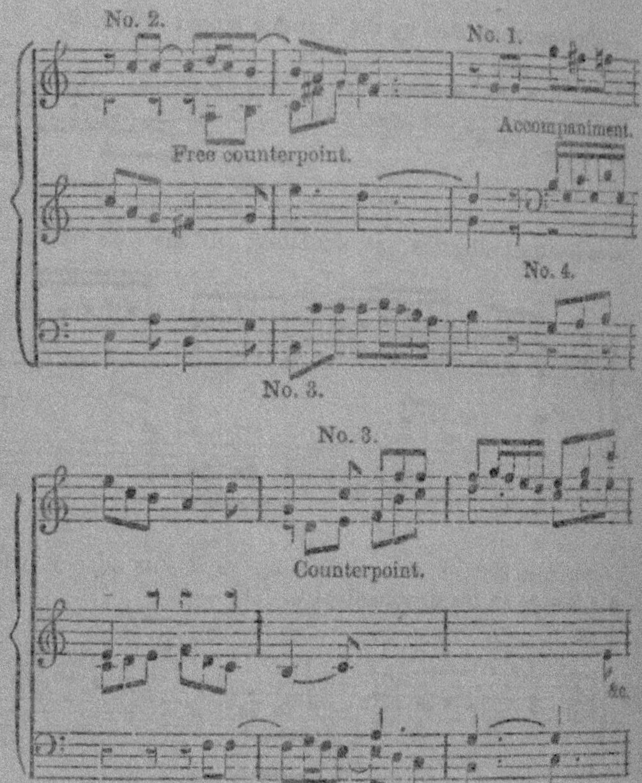


To follow out the ramifications of the fugue to the end, with its sequences, episodes, and other devices of counterpoint, would be to little purpose. It is entirely constructed upon the foregoing materials. An episode immediately preceding the *coda*, in which the opening bar of the first of the four themes is first given by inversion, and answered direct:—

—afterwards imitated by the first and second violins :—

—will attract attention ; so, doubtless, will the *coda* itself :—

—which is carried on as brilliantly as it sets out ; so wil the passage on the dominant pedal (G) :—

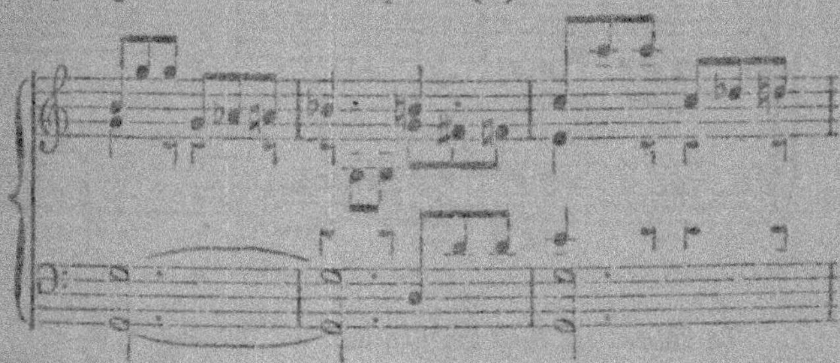

—and so the snatches from all four themes :—

—leading to the vigorous unison for all the instruments, with which a movement almost unique in its kind is brought to an end:

Francis Joseph Haydn was born on the 21st of March, 1732, at Rhorau, and died on the 31st of May, 1809,* at Vienna, in his 79th year. Long as he lived, his productions are so numerous that they might reasonably account for a still more protracted career. The catalogue of his works which he drew up with his own hand, and presented to Carpani for the *Memoirs*, comprises upwards of eight hundred compositions of more or less importance. Besides his oratorios and masses, so well known to all musicians and amateurs in this country, Haydn composed twenty-four operas, one hundred and eighteen orchestral symphonies, and eighty-three quartets for stringed instruments. If he had written nothing but his quartets, he would have done quite enough—without oratorio, mass, opera, symphony, or canzonet—to render himself immortal. The number of his compositions for the chamber is prodigious, and as a whole they constitute one of the most varied and precious bequests to the art. They are otherwise interesting, moreover, for two special reasons; first, because the earlier examples exercised an undoubted influence in directing the studies and in forming the genius of Mozart; and, secondly, because the best of them show an ambition on the part of one who had been the model, and in a certain sense the master, to emulate the greatness of his still more gifted pupil and successor. It is an incident unique in the history of music, that Haydn, to whom Mozart owed so much, should afterwards have repaid himself with interest, by borrowing from the very source to which he had originally contributed. Every amateur knows what Mozart thought of Haydn; and every amateur equally knows what Haydn thought of Mozart.

* The year of Mendelssohn's birth, and fifty years subsequent to the death of Handel.

## SONG, Mr. GREAVES.

(*Orlando.*) *Handel.*

Lascia Amor, è siegui Marte;
Va, combatti per la gloria.
Sol oblio quel ti comparte,
Questo sol bella memoria.

---

SONATA, in D minor, Op. 29 (or 31), No. 2, for Pianoforte alone.* *Beethoven.*

(Tenth performance at the Popular Concerts.)

Allegro—D minor.
Adagio—B flat major.
Allegretto—D minor.

Madlle. MARIE KREBS.

Though this sonata contains no *scherzo*, or minuet, it is as fully entitled to the conventional appellation, "Grand," as either of its companions. In originality it yields to no previous or subsequent work of Beethoven. The first movement is remarkable for the introduction of an element of effect wholly new to this class of composition; for while examples of what is termed "recitative" may be met with in some of the fantasias of J. S. Bach (who seems to have anticipated almost everything), there is no instance of it in a pianoforte sonata anterior to the one under notice. The leading subject of the first movement is divided into two sections, the one *largo*, the other *allegro*; and as both play an important part in its development, they are submitted in *extenso*:—

* No. 17 of Beethoven's Sonatas, edited by Mr. CHARLES HALLÉ —Published by CHAPPELL and Co. 50, New Bond Street.

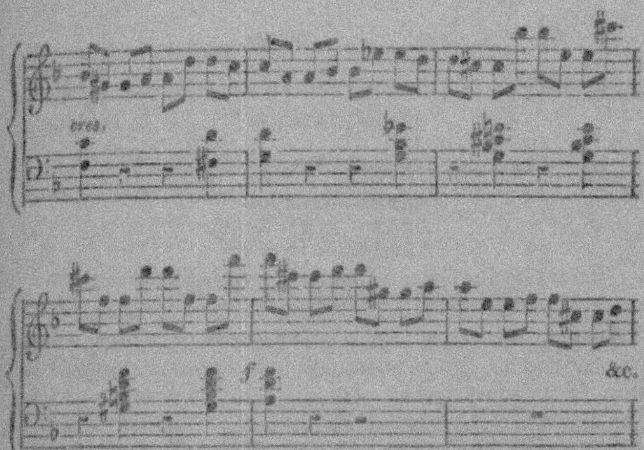


The first section (the *largo*) generates, among other features, the "recitative" to which allusion has been made; the second (the *allegro*) is the chief means of investing the movement with that impassioned character which everywhere pervades it, and which appears to be a frequent idiosyncracy of Beethoven in the key of D minor.* When a full close is attained, a subsidiary in the same key presents itself—half made up of the first section of the leading subject, and half of an entirely new melody:—

The development of the foregoing leads to the dominant of A minor, and at the same time to the second subject, the agitated character of which is in thorough keeping:—

* Witness the slow movements of the Quartet in F (Op. 18), of the Pianoforte Sonata in D major (Op. 10), and of the Trio in D major (Op. 70)—to say nothing of the unparalleled first *allegro* of the Ninth Symphony.

Retarding the full cadence in his accustomed manner, the composer introduces a new subject before allowing the ear to repose :—

As if impatient of remaining for more than an instant in the key, however, Beethoven now turns this passionate phrase to good account, accomplishing through its means one of the transitions to which he is so partial :—

—his sudden return to the key (A minor) which he has thus unceremoniously quitted, being just as signal a characteristic of his manner. Once planted surely on the *terra firma* of A minor, we have again an entirely new theme, in (free) double counterpoint :—

The alteration of C to A, and of D to B (**) when the florid subject falls to the left hand, is to avoid "consecutive octaves" between treble and bass. This new theme is the peroration which conducts the first part of the first movement to an end. The second part begins, at once, with a specimen of the "recitative" of which mention has been made, and which, it will be perceived, springs out of the few notes of *largo* (quoted) constituting the first section of the leading subject :—

A recurrence of this, in a different key, after another pause, leads eventually to F sharp, in the minor of which the subsidiary theme (already described) :—

is repeated. The elaborations of the second part, until we arrive at a new pedal passage on the dominant of D minor, are exclusively built upon the foregoing materials. After this, a more lengthened application of the recitative is presented—as subjoined :—

Impressive, nevertheless, as such a resumption of the leading theme appears, Beethoven, apparently unsatisfied, aims at something more. After the pause (*adagio*) which interrupts the *allegro* at the end of four bars (see first quotation), some further recitative, quite of a dramatic cast :—

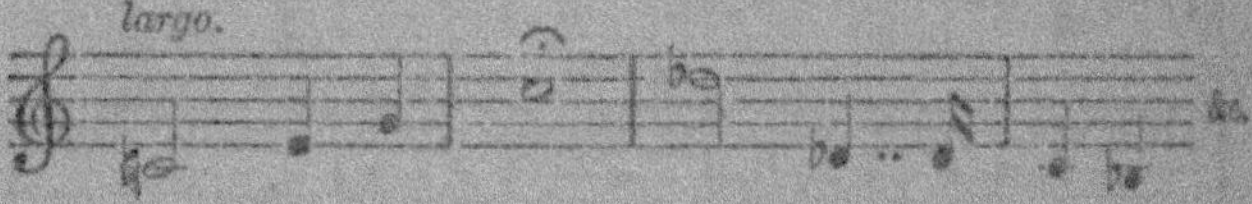


—leads, through an enharmonic progression, to the following episode :—

This, however, is speedily arrested by the unexpected reappearance of the second subject in D minor; in which key—after the customary recapitulation and a brief *coda*—the movement is brought to an end, "*pianissimo.*"

The *adagio* (B flat major) has something in common with the slow movement of the Fourth Symphony, although the resemblance is rather in the impression left on the mind than in any great similarity of subject or treatment. The leading theme affords exquisite relief to the stormy passion of the *allegro*:—

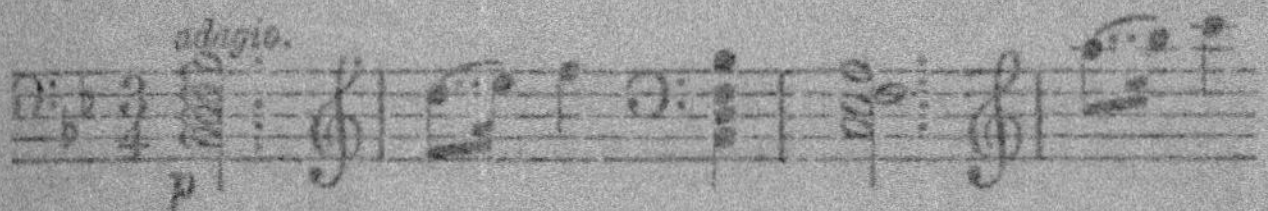


The sentiment of tranquility prevails from one end of this *adagio* to the other. Take the continuation of the opening as an instance:—

—and the exquisite melody which, after the foregoing has been richly developed on the dominant pedal (C), steals forth in F major, thus unobtrusively:—

Even the variation of the leading theme, subsequent to its reappearance, with fuller harmony—though difficult to execute with the necessary repose—does not in any sense militate against the prevalent tone of quietude:—

When this variation has been brought to a full close, in B flat, the bass note becomes the dominant harmony of another key (E flat):—

in which the continuation of the principal is recapitulated; the dominant pedal now resting upon F, and the second subject recurring in B flat. A fresh pedal passage—still richer and even more beautiful than its predecessor:—

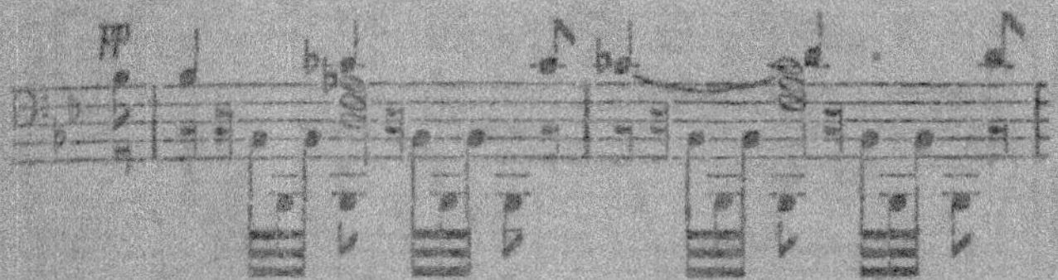

carries us back once more to the leading theme, now presented in a modified form; while the brief *coda*, on a tonic pedal (B flat), introducing the subjoined stately melodic phrase:—

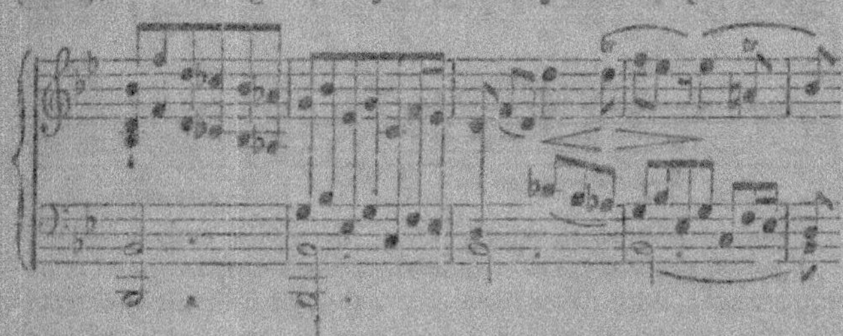

brings the *adagio* to an end with a repose as exquisite as that which marks its commencement. This, like its immediate precursor, is a movement eminently *Beethovenian.* Not less so is the *finale* (*allegretto*), which, in spite of its more brilliant character, is as full of passion and sentiment as the *allegro* itself. Here we are again plunged into the gloom of the minor—from which we only obtain relief at intervals, through "fits and starts" of brief duration. The leading subject (probably on account of the prevalence of one "figure" throughout the movement) has been frequently charged with a resemblance to the *finale* of Mozart's pianoforte sonata in A minor; but the comparison is forced, and to refute it by quotation would be superfluous. The subjoined indicates the prominent character of Beethoven's *Allegretto*:

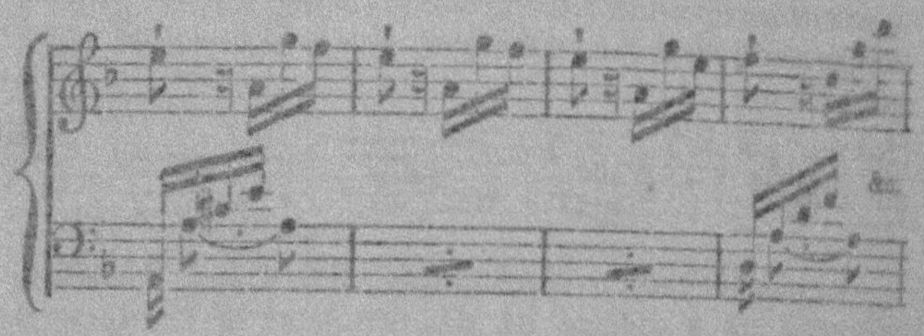

The close is thus prolonged (the accompaniment may be imagined) :—

—the recurrence to which point, near the end, is one of the most original ideas of the whole movement.

The second subject (in A minor) is even more agitated and impassioned than the first. The melody alone will suffice to indicate its character :—

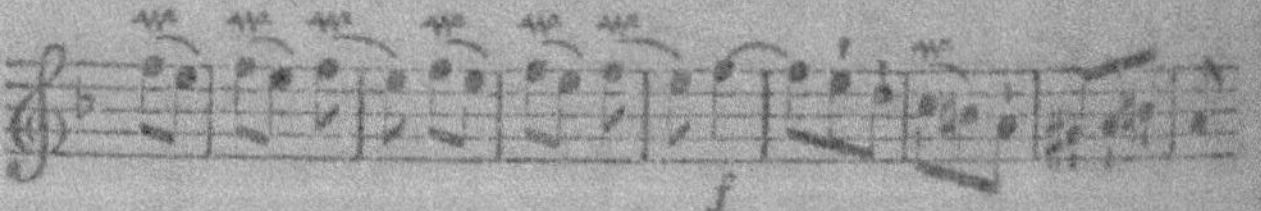


When this is fully worked out, we have a peroration in the same key :—

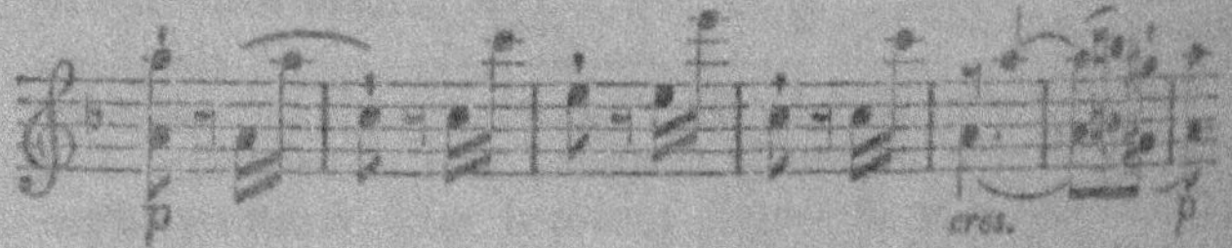


the development of which is arrested by a new passage, leading to a repetition of the first part. The elaborations of the second part—commencing with a quasi-inversion of the principal subject :—

—are exclusively constructed upon the leading theme. Among other beautiful ideas thus generated, one is particularly worth attention :—

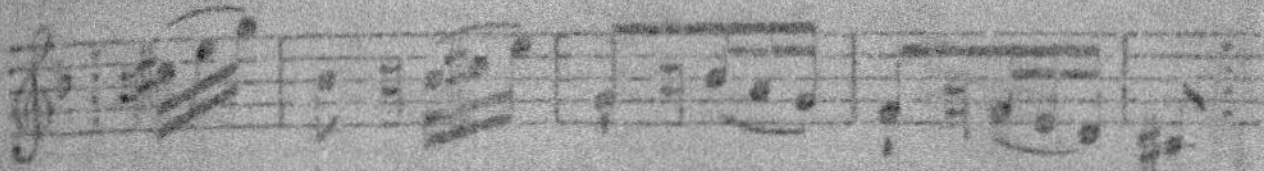

The very interesting development of this new thought is interrupted by a cadence on the dominant of the original key :—

—leading back to the principal subject, the course of which is now varied by a singularly beautiful transition, of which an outline is subjoined :—

After some recapitulation, the second subject comes back, in D minor (instead of A minor). This is developed in the new key, as at first, the final appearance of the leading theme, however, being arrested by the "quasi-inversion" (already cited), now very materially extended and developed. The principal subject is at length resumed, with fresh modifications, to enhance its effect :—

The prolongation of the full close already cited, is now itself developed in a striking and original manner:—

An extremely short *coda*, built upon a fragment of the leading theme, brings this truly magnificent sonata—which might have been designated *Sonata Dramatica* with even better reason than the "Op. 13" *Sonata Patetica*—to a brilliant and effective conclusion.

According to Schindler, Beethoven's friend and biographer, the theme of this last movement was suggested to the composer by a man on horseback galloping past his window. The peculiarity of its rhythm certainly gives credit to the statement.

The three sonatas Op. 31 (Op. 29 is the string quintet in C) were composed about 1802.

The Sonata in D minor was first introduced by Mr. Charles Hallé, at the first concert of the sixth season—November 2, 1863.

---

*** Madlle. MARIE KREBS will perform on one of Messrs. JOHN BROADWOOD and SONS' Concert Grand Pianofortes.

SATURDAY POPULAR CONCERTS, ST. JAMES'S HALL.—On Saturday afternoon, January 30, the Programme will include Brahms' Quartet in A major, Op. 26, for Pianoforte and Strings; Mozart's Quartet in E flat, for Strings; Chopin's Sonata in G major, Op. 65, for Pianoforte and Violoncello; and Beethoven's Air with Variations, in F major, Op. 34, for Pianoforte alone. Executants, Madame NORMAN-NÉRUDA, MM. HANS VON BÜLOW, STRAUS, L. RIES, and PIATTI. Vocalist, Signor FEDERICI. Conductor, Sir JULIUS BENEDICT. To commence at Three o'Clock.

Subscription Tickets, to the Sofa Stalls, for the 7 Morning Concerts, taking place on Saturdays, January 16, 23, 30, February 6, 13, 20, and 27, at £1 10s.

Sofa Stalls, 5s. Balcony, 3s. Admission, 1s. Tickets and Programmes at CHAPPELL & Co.'s, 50, New Bond Street.

# Entr' Acte.

---

## QUEEN ISABELLA'S PIANO.

*"Se non è vero," etc.*

When Serrano was Regent of Spain, among the *on dits* that passed current was the following:—

Madame Serrano, as wife of the Regent, occupied the apartments in the royal palace of the ex-queen, and no doubt she was well pleased with her residence, for the rooms were most luxuriantly furnished. But soon after the Regent's occupancy of the palace, Isabella demanded the restitution of such of her private property as it contained, and the Spanish nation was in nowise disposed to withhold anything from her that she could justly lay claim to; all was to be forwarded to her, to the very last article. Load after load of boxes and bales were carried to the depôt, to be forwarded to Isabella by rail, and among the articles sent there were not a few that the new occupants of the palace were sorry to be deprived of. After a time the ex-Queen made a demand for several things that were wanting, especially for a piano with which a musical association of which she had been the patroness had presented her.

The instrument was very richly ornamented with gold, and bore on the front side a beautiful medallion set with diamonds. It was—said Isabella, when she left Madrid for a watering-place near the French line—in her private apartments. But Mdme. Serrano knew nothing of—had not seen it—and the whole palace was ransacked for the lost piano, yet it was nowhere to be found. The dethroned queen, however, insisted that the "valued souvenir" should be restored to her. The consequence was, that the situation became embarrassing for Serrano *vis-à-vis* of his afore-time patroness, and all the more so as it was said that the piano was in the late queen's apartments when the Serrano family moved into them. Serrano even hunted through the palace himself for the lost instrument, and, although Mdme Serrano assured him that it was not in her rooms, he included them in his search, being haunted by a dim recollection that he had seen it somewhere. Finally, his threats and entreaties drew from his consort the humiliating confession that she, in a momentary pecuniary embarrassment, had sold the piano. The scene that followed in the Serrano household is said to have been more animated than edifying: but the regent knew now, at least, where to look for the missing "souvenir," which was a great point gained.

He immediately sent a confidential agent to the purchaser in order to buy it back again; but—O monstrous!—the instrument had already become so demoralised, so plebeian, as to be the inmate of a coffee-house, after having been robbed of its costly ornamentation of gold and diamonds, which had been disposed of to a jeweller. What was to be done? The *chronique scandaleuse* of Madrid had already taken up the subject, and therefore there was no time to be lost. Serrano's agent repaired to the coffee-house, and offered double the sum for the piano that had been paid for it; but the cunning landlord declared he could not do without it, and consented to part with it only when five times the sum was offered him.

Now the jeweller was hunted up, and he was found to have as sharp an eye to business as the coffee-house man. He expressed a thousand regrets that he had already melted up the gold and disposed of the diamonds; he added, however, that it would be possible to reproduce the ornamentation even to the smallest detail, as, on account of the beauty of its design, he had made a cateful sketch of it. This statement looked rather improbable; but the piano must be forthcoming, cost what it would, and that, too, exactly in its original dress, in order to avoid the threatened scandal. The jeweller's demands were acceded to, and in a remarkably short space of time the instrument, carefully packed, was returned to the palace, where it was said to have been finally discovered in an out-of-the-way corner, together with other of the ex-queen's personal belongings.

When the fearfully misused piano, which had cost the Regent so much money, and caused him so much trouble, was finally forwarded to its owner, he felt greatly relieved. And the piano, however much out of tune, probably found its wonted harmony sooner than did the little domestic circle in which it had created such discord.—*Musical World.*

---

## SONATA, in A, Op. 104, for Pianoforte and Violoncello. *Hummel.*

(First performance at the Popular Concerts.)

Allegro cantabile grazioso—A major.
Romanza, un poco adagio e con espressione—C major.
Rondo—allegro, vivace un poco—A minor.

### Madlle. MARIE KREBS and Signor PIATTI.

Though one of Hummel's latest compositions, this sonata is also one of his most symmetrically constructed. The three movements, one and all, are so clear and concise, that a brief extract from the leading themes of each will answer all purposes:—

*Allegro cantabile* (first theme—melody only).

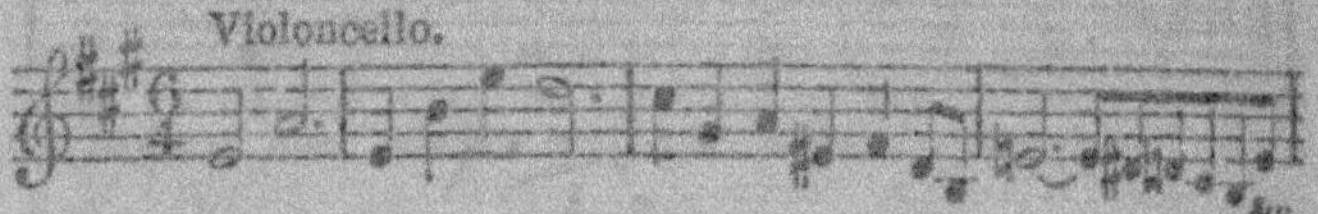


The pianoforte continues the theme, as below:—

(*Bravura* Passage.)

(Episode—C major.)

The second theme now appears in a more ornate and florid shape :—

This being developed at some length, a sudden transition brings us to the key of E (the dominant of the primary):—

—and in this key the first part of the *allegro* (which is repeated) comes to an end.

The movement is constructed upon these materials almost exclusively, allowing for an episode at the beginning of the second part, in which the violoncello has an important share:—

The second subject returns in D major—answered, as before, by the violoncello:—

(Theme and answer only.)

Shortly after, the leading theme comes back in the primary key:—

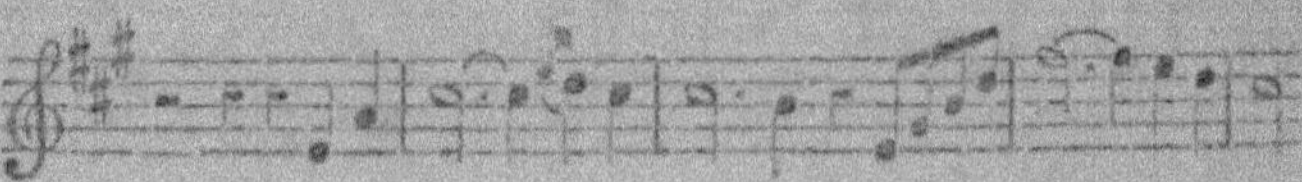

Then follows a reference to the *bravura* passage, already cited (page 593) :—

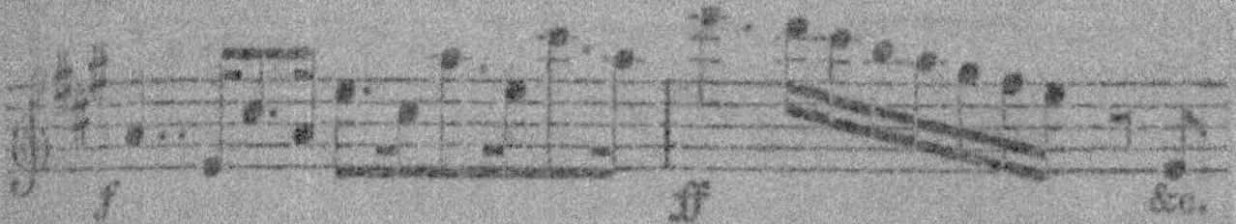


The second subject also, according to traditional use, reappears in the primary :—

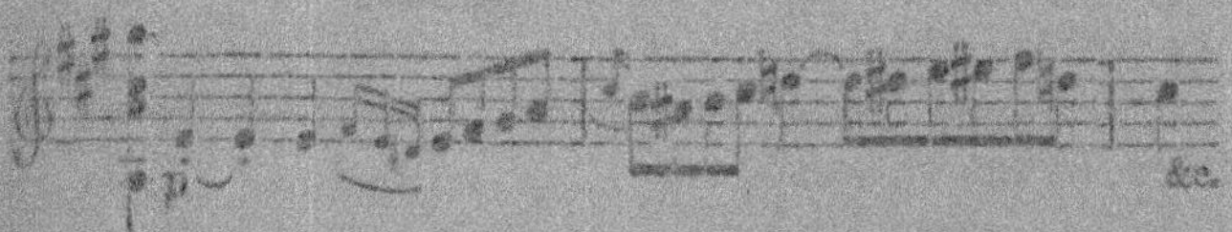


—and the first episode (see page 594) is heard again. A brief allusion to the *coda,* which brings the movement to an end, will suffice :—

—with the addition of a few bars from the peroration, which terminates the second, as it terminates the first part of the movement :—

A very few quotations from the *Romanza* will suffice:—

(Leading theme.)

(Episode—C minor.)

We have now the refrain of the leading theme repeated in E flat major :—

To this succeeds a repetition of the leading theme in the primary key (C major), given to the violoncello, with a new accompaniment for the pianoforte, which may speak for itself :—

(Theme—melody only.)

The *adagio* comes peacefully to an end with the Refrain already twice cited :—

The *finale*, in the minor key, and in the *rondo* form, is, perhaps, more charateristic of Hummel than either of the preceding movements. In some of his concertos he has given admirable specimens of this peculiar form, and in the present instance he may be said to be in his happiest vein.

(Leading theme.)

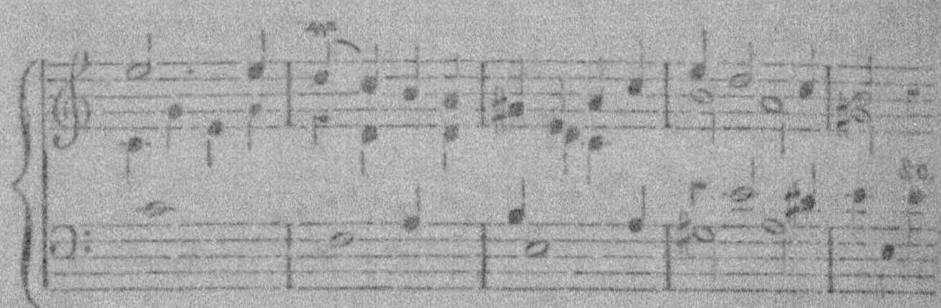


(Peroration to leading theme.)

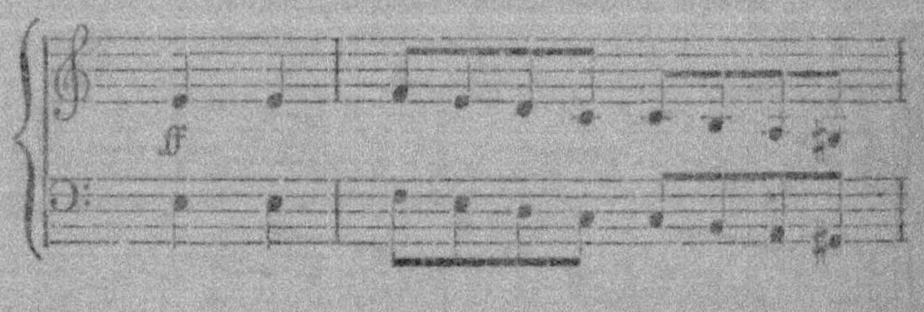

(Preamble to second theme, in the dominant of C major.)

(Second theme.)

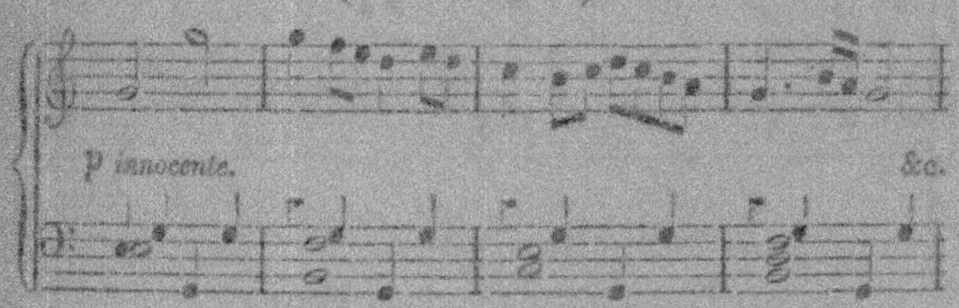


*Bravura* (peroration to second theme).

After an episode, considerably developed, the leading theme returns in the primary key; and we have then a brilliant *coda*, commencing as below:—

—and finishing in the same style:—

JOHANN NEPOMEK HUMMEL was born November 14, 1778, at Presburg, where his father was music master in the military school of Wartberg. At the age of four he learned to play the violin, but without evincing a decided bias for music. The next year he began to take lessons in singing, and on the piano. From that time his faculties were rapidly developed, and in a single year he acquired remarkable skill. His father removed to Vienna, and became *chef-d'orchestre* in Schikaneder's theatre, where little Hummel, scarcely seven years old, attracted the attention of Mozart and other distinguished artists. Mozart, in spite of his repugnance to giving lessons, offered to take charge of the boy's musical education, provided he would live with him, and be always near him. Of course the proposition was gratefully accepted. With such a master, Hummel made prodigious progress, and, at the age of nine, excited the admiration of all who heard him.

His father then thought to turn his precocious talent to account, and they travelled through Germany, Denmark, and Scotland. Hummel's first public appearance was in a concert at Dresden, 1787. He next played before the court at Cassel. At Edinburgh the child pianist created great enthusiasm; and there he published his first work, a theme with variations, dedicated to the Queen of England. After spending the years 1791 and 1792 in London, he visited Holland, and then returned to Vienna.

Hummel was now fifteen years old, and his execution might already be considered the most correct and brilliant of the German school. Meanwhile his studies became more serious than before. His father, who was excessively severe, exacted incessant labour from him; and when Hummel had become a man and a famous artist, he was still subject to that will. At Vienna he studied harmony, accompaniment, and counterpoint with Albrechtsberger, and formed a friendship with Salieri, who gave him useful hints about singing and the dramatic style. In 1803 he entered the service of Prince Esterhazy, and composed his first Mass, which won the approbation of Haydn. About the same time he wrote ballets and operas for the theatres of Vienna, which were favourably received. Although only twenty-eight years old, his works (especially his instrumental music), and his fine talent for execution, had rendered him famous in Germany; but his name was absolutely unknown in France until the year 1806, when Cherubini brought home from Vienna the Grand Fantasia in E flat (Op. 18), which was executed at the *concours* of the Conservatory that same year, and, although only understood by artists, so raised Hummel's reputation in Paris that all the pianists sought his works.

In 1811, Hummel left the service of Prince Esterhazy, and until 1816 had no other employment than that of professor of the piano, at Vienna. Then for four years he held the place of chapel-master to the King of Wurtemburg, and afterwards entered the service of the Grand Duke of Weimar, in the same capacity. Two years later he obtained leave of absence to make an artistic tour in Russia. St. Petersburg and Moscow gave him the most brilliant reception. In 1823 he went through Holland and Belgium, and finally to Paris, where his success was worthy of his talent. His improvisations on the piano excited the liveliest admiration. Returning to Weimar, which place he did not leave until 1827, he heard of the approaching end of Beethoven, between whom and himself there had been some unpleasant differences.

Hastening to the bedside of the dying composer, Hummel could not repress his tears; Beethoven held out his hand, they embraced, and all was forgotten.

Two years afterwards, Hummel again visited Paris and London; but his playing did not produce the same sensation as before. After a journey to Poland, he passed the remainder of his days peacefully at Weimar, and died on the 17th of October, 1827, at the age of fifty-nine.

Hummel was equally distinguished as a performer (on the piano), improvisatore, and composer. In execution, continuing the pure style of Mozart, enhanced by the regular principles of mechanism which he learned of Clementi during two years in London, he became himself the founder of a new German school, in which many celebrated artists have been formed. The epoch of Hummel among the German pianists was a real epoch of progress and of transformation. Greater difficulties have been conquered, greater power and sonority of tone have been produced in piano playing since his time; but no one has gone beyond him in purity, regularity, and correctness of execution, in crispness of touch, in colouring and expression. His performance was less the result of a desire to display great skill than the attempt to express thoughts essentially musical. These thoughts, always complete, manifested themselves under his hands with all the advantages of grace, delicacy, depth, and expression.

In his improvisations, Hummel had such power of fixing and giving regular form to his fugitive ideas and inspirations that he seemed to be executing premeditated compositions. And yet there was nothing cold or mechanical; the ideas were so felicitous, the manner so charming, the details so elegant, that his hearers were lost in admiration.

Hummel's very remarkable productions, especially in the sphere of instrumental music, have placed him in the first rank of distinguished composers of the nineteenth century. General opinion has hardly estimated his best works highly enough. His Septuor in D minor (Op. 74); his Quintet for piano (Op. 87); his Concertos in A minor (Op. 85), in B minor (Op. 89), in E major (Op. 110), and in A flat (Op. 113); some of his trios for piano, violin, and violoncello; the solo sonatas in F minor (Op. 20), and D major (Op. 106), are works of the very highest merit—in short, more or less masterpieces. As a composer of Church music, Hummel also holds a high rank; his masses standing in some respects (though, of course, inferior to those of Beethoven and Cherubini) nearest to those of Haydn and Mozart.

The works of Hummel have been classed as follows:—

I. *Dramatic Music*—"*Le Vicende d' Amore,*" comic opera in two acts. 2. "*Mathilde de Guise,*" opera in three acts. 3. "*Das Haus ist zu verkaufen,*" in one act. "*Die Rückfahrt des Kaisers,*" in one act. 5. "*Eloge de l'Amitié,*" cantata with choruses. 6. "*Diana ed Endimione,*" an Italian cantata with orchestra. 7. "*Hélène et Paris,*" ballet. 8. "*Sappho de Mytilène,*" ditto. 9. "*Le Tableau Parlant,*" ditto. 10. "*L' Anneau Magique,*" pantomime, with singing and dances. 11. "*Le Combat Magique,* ditto.

II. *Church Music* —1. Mass for four voices, with orchestra and organ, in B flat (Op. 77). 2. Second Mass, in B flat (Op. 80). 3. Third Mass, in D (Op. 111). 4. Gradual (*Quodquod in orbe*), for four voices, orchestra, and organ (Op. 88). 5. Offertory (*Alma Virgo*), for soprano solo, chorus, orchestra and organ (Op. 89).

III. *Instrumental Music*—1. Overture for grand orchestra, in B flat (Op. 101). 2. Three string quartets (Op. 30). 3 and 4, Grand Serenade, for piano, guitar, clarionet, and bassoon, Nos. I. and II. (Op. 63 and 66). 5. Grand Septuor, in D minor, for piano, flute, oboe, horn, alto, violoncello, and double bass (Op. 74). 7. Grand Military Septuor, in C, for piano, flute, violin, clarionet, trumpet, and double bass (Op. 114). 8. Symphony Concertante, for piano and violin (Op. 17). 9. Concerto for piano, in C (Op. 34). 10. Easy Concerto for piano, in G (Op. 73) 11. Third Concerto, in A minor (Op. 85). 12. Fourth Concerto, in B minor (Op. 89). 13. "*Les Adieux,*" Fifth Concerto, in E major (Op. 110). 14. Sixth Concerto, in A flat (Op. 113). 15. Brilliant Rondos for piano and orchestra (Op. 56, 98, and 117). 16. Thêmes variés for piano and orchestra (Op. 56, 98, and 117). 17. "*Le Cor enchanté d' Obéron,*" grand fantasia for piano and orchestra, in E major (Op. 116). 18. Trios for piano, violin, and violoncello (Op. 12, 22, 35, 65, 83, 93, 66). 19. Sonatas for piano and violin (Op. 5, 19, 25, 23, 37, 50, 64, 104). 20. Sonatas for piano, with four hands (Op. 43, 92, 99). 21. Sonatas for piano alone (Op. 13, 20, 36, 81, 106). 22. Detached pieces for piano solo, viz., three Fugues (Op. 7); Rondos (Op 11, 19, 107, 109); Fantasias (Op. 18, 123, 124); *Etudes and Caprices* (Op. 49, 67, 105, 125); Variations (Op. 1, 2, 8, 9, 40, 57, 118, 119), &c. 23. Complete Method, theoretic and practical, for the piano.

In the above catalogue, compiled by M. Fétis, the Seventh Pianoforte Concerto (in F major), the Quintet, Op. 87 (in E flat), and other important works, are omitted.

---

## SONG, Mr. GREAVES. *Buononcini.*

Love leads to battle—who dares oppose him?
 The rebel squadrons his presence fly;
See how the hero drives all before him,
 Armed with lightning shot from her eye.

Victory, glory, to love the conqueror!
 Hear his brave soldiers in trumph cry.
Where are his enemies? fallen before him;
 In silken fetters they captive lie.

Giovanni Battista Buononcini was a native of Modena. The comparative merits of Handel and Buononcini became the subject of violent disputes in fashionable circles. The Italian composer, though far inferior to his illustrious rival, was a man of great merit, and had a large body of warm partisans. Swift, who bestows a passing lash on many of the follies of his day, ridiculed the dissentions on this subject in the following doggrel:—

"Some say that Signor Buononcini
Compared to Handel's a mere ninny;
While others say that, to him Handel
Is hardly fit to hold a candle.
Strange that such difference should be
'Twixt tweedle-dum and tweedle-dee!"

Buononcini's "*Griselda*," the best opera he produced in this country, was brought out in 1722, and had a very great run. The drama (founded on the well-known legend) was written by Rolli; "the airs"—says a writer of the last century—"are full of elegance and expression, and the accompaniments contain excellent instrumental effects, especially for oboes."

---

SONATA, in E flat, Op. 12, No. 3, for Pianoforte and Violin. *Beethoven.*

(Sixth performance at the Popular Concerts.)

Allegro con spirito—E flat major.
Adagio con molto espressione—C major.
Rondo, allegro molto—E flat major.

Madlle. MARIE KRBES and
Madame NORMAN-NÉRUDA.

The three sonatas, Op. 12, were composed about 1799—between the trio in B flat, for piano, clarionet (or violin), and violoncello, and the famous solo-sonata generally known as the "*Sonate Pathétique.*" They were dedicated to the Italian composer, Salieri,* the rival of Mozart in the graces of the Imperial Court at Vienna, and from whom Beethoven himself, as well as Schubert and Hummel, received hints about dramatic composition.† The other two sonatas, Op. 12, are in D and

---

* "*Tre sonate per il clavicembalo, o fortepiano, con un violino dedicate al Signore A. Salieri.*" (Original title.)

† The incredible "tradition" of Salieri having poisoned Mozart out of artistic jealousy is now universally scouted. Even Oulibischeff rejects it:—"Among the Italian composers at Vienna," says Mozart's biographer, "there are some who saw far enough into the future to feel convinced that Mozart would ultimately be their ruin; that his German Opera was the first blow dealt at the universal supremacy of Italian music, and that these German barbarians would end by wresting the musical sceptre from their hands. Of all the instances of hate and enmity towards the great man, however, only one has become historical; that of Salieri, a pupil of Gluck, and a more learned musician than any other operatic composer among his own countrymen. Salieri was naturally Mozart's most implacable foe. The flattering error of judgment which caused the Parisians to mistake Salieri's opera, *Die Danaïden* for the composition of Gluck, his position of first *Capellmeister* at the Imperial court, his great reputation, and his many dramatic triumphs, all combined to increase his hatred of a young man, who, though without official title or appointment, and a poor music master, Salieri, could not fail to perceive, surpassed him as he surpassed every one else. If we are to believe a tradition which, even at the present day, finds an echo in some breasts, Salieri rendered himself infamous by a dreadful act. According to the report, he poisoned Mozart. Luckily for the honour of the Italian musician, this tradition is as destitute of foundation as of probability; as stupid as it is horrible; ("*Life of Mozart,*" translated by J. V. Bridgeman, for the *Musical World.*) M. Oulibischeff, nevertheless, insists upon the fact that the wretched performance of *Figaro*, on its first representation at Vienna, before Joseph II and his court, was entirely owing to the intrigues of Salieri with the Italian singers, against Mozart, and in favour of

B flat. The first criticism upon these works which appeared in the *Allegemeine Musik-Zeitung* is worth citing :—

"Gelehrte Masse ohne gute Methode—keine Natur, kein Gesang, ein Wald wo man durch feindliche Verhau alle Augenblicke auf gehalten, erschöpft, ohne Freude herauskommt. Ein Anhaüfen von Schwerigkeit auf Schwerigkeit, das man alle Geduld verliere. Wenn Beethoven sich nur mehr *selbst* verlaügnen und den Gang der Natur einschlagen wollte; so könnte er bei seinem Talente und Fleisse uns sicher rechter viel Guter liefern."*

Opinions, however, have changed since then, and many a school-girl is now able to appreciate, if not to execute with fluency and correctness, what seemed so ungrateful to the learned critic of the *Allegemeine Musik-Zeitung.*

The leading subjects of the various movements of the sonata in E flat are subjoined :—

*Allegro con spirito.*

Martini and his *Cosa Rara*. The report of the poisoning had attained such currency, that, thirty-four years afterwards (1825, at Vienna), when on his death bed, Salieri solemnly declared his innocence. All that is known of his character, moreover, tends to show the utter absurdity of the accusations. Salieri, at various intervals, was master in the art of dramatic composition to Weigl, Beethoven, Schubert, and Meyerbeer.

* "A mass of learned things, without method; no nature, no song—a forest, in which one is arrested, at every step, by hostile thickets, from which one issues exhausted, without pleasure; a heaping up of difficulties upon difficulties, till one's patience is exhausted. If Beethoven would deny himself, and enter into the paths of nature, he might, with his talent, and his love for work, produce many excellent things" (!).

(Second theme.)
&c.
(Episode in second part.)

&c.
p legato.
sf p
(Episode.)
Violin.
p

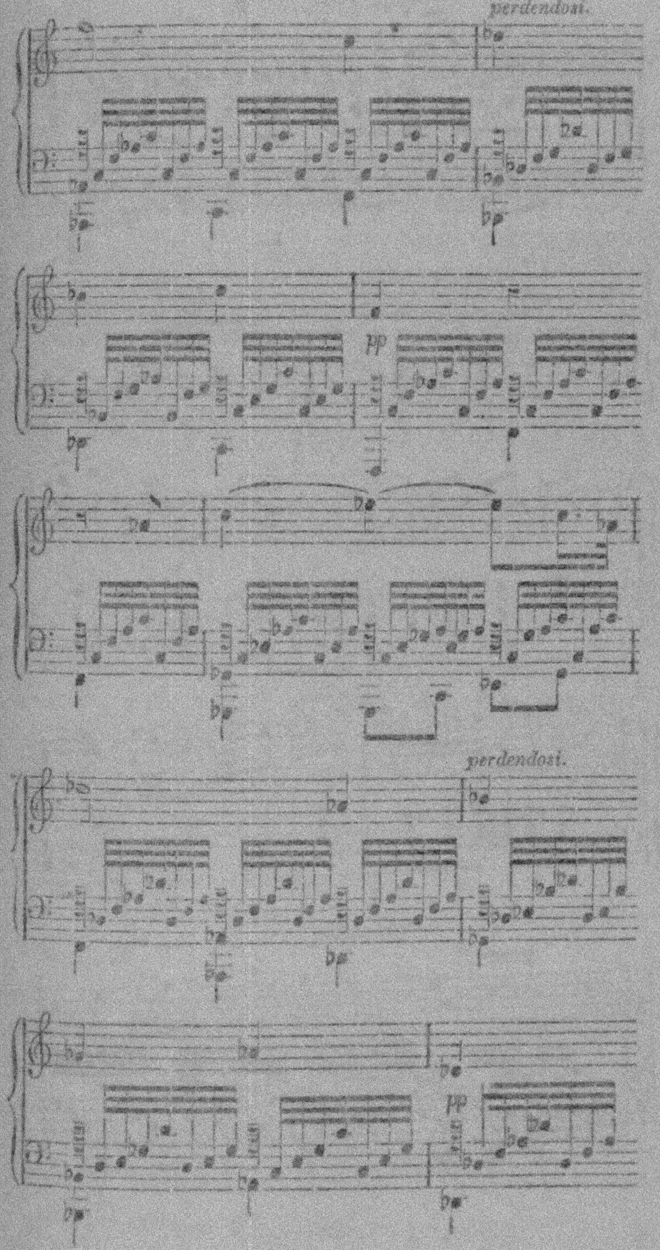
perdendosi.
pp
pp
perdendosi.
pp

*Rondo, allegro molto.*

&c.
(Episode.)
Violin.
sf
sf
sf
&c.
(Coda.)
p

Although a very early work, this sonata bears the true stamp of Beethoven.

The Sonata in E flat was first introduced by Madame Arabella Goddard and M. Sainton, at the ninth concert of the fourth season—Feb. 3rd, 1862.

---

END OF THE FIVE HUNDRED AND FIRST CONCERT.

---

J. MALLETT, PRINTER, 59, WARDOUR STREET, SOHO, LONDON.

# MONDAY POPULAR CONCERTS.

MONDAY EVENING, JANUARY 25th, 1875.

## PROGRAMME.

### PART I.

QUARTET, in G major, Op. 54, No. 2, for two Violins, Viola, and Violoncello ............................................ *Haydn.*

Madame NORMAN-NÉRUDA,
MM. L. RIES, STRAUS, and PIATTI.

SONGS, { "Waldeinsamkeit" / "Die Waldhexe." } ................................ *Rubinstein.*

Miss ANTOINETTE STERLING.

SONATA, in D major, Op. 10, No. 3, for Pianoforte alone... *Beethoven.*

Madlle. MARIE KREBS.

### PART II.

TRIO, in G minor, for Pianoforte, Violin, and Violoncello...... *Chopin.*

(First time at the Popular Concerts)

Madlle. MARIE KREBS, Madame NORMAN-NÉRUDA, and Signor PIATTI.

SONGS, { "Die Letzte Hoffnung." / "Der Tod und das Mädchen." / "Auf dem Wasser zu singen." } ...................... *Schubert.*

Miss ANTOINETTE STERLING.

SONATA, in G major (No. 11 of Hallé's Edition), for Pianoforte and Violin ...................................... *Mozart.*

Madlle. KREBS and Madame NORMAN-NÉRUDA.

Conductor - - Mr. ZERBINI.

4 Z

www.ingramcontent.com/pod-product-compliance
Lightning Source LLC
Chambersburg PA
CBHW081215170626
46811CB00010B/3302

* 9 7 8 1 5 3 5 8 1 0 7 6 0 *